THE WEST TEXAS CHILI MONSTER

by Judy Cox

illustrated by John O'Brien

BridgeWater Books

For Tim and Christopher
—J.C.

For Tess
—J.O.

Text copyright © 1998 by Judy Cox.
Illustrations copyright © 1998 by John O'Brien.

Published by BridgeWater Books, an imprint and registered trademark
of Troll Communications L.L.C.

Produced by Boingo Books, Inc.

Printed in the United States of America.

10 9 8 7 6 5 4 3 2

Library of Congress Cataloging-in-Publication Data

Cox, Judy.
The West Texas chili monster / by Judy Cox; illustrated by John O'Brien.
p.   cm.
Summary: Unexpected things happen when Mama's rip-roarin', rootin'-tootin', rip-snortin' chili
attracts a space monster to the West Texas chili contest.
ISBN 0-8167-4546-3
[1. Chili con carne—Fiction. 2. Contests—Fiction. 3. Extraterrestrial beings—Fiction. 4. Texas—Fiction.]
I. O'Brien, John, 1953-   ill. II. Title.
PZ7.C83835Wf   1998
[E]— dc21   97-34303

Out in the West Texas town of Que Pasa, where the sky's so big it touches the ground, there lived a widow lady called Mama. Mama made the bestest chili in the whole of Que Pasa—maybe the whole state of Texas.

Tuesday was chili night at Mama's ranch. The smell of simmering chili brought coyotes down from the hills and jackrabbits up from the hollows.

Folks moseyed in from nearly everywhere. From the lobster coasts of Maine and the rainy plains of Spain they came, just for a bite of Mama's chili.

When that supper bell rang, Mama's six young'uns came running. Up from the gulches where they scrabbled for horned toads, down from the hayloft where they hunted for kittens, Inez, Lorenzo, Isabel, Alfonse, Alma, and Baby came.

They'd never be late for Mama's chili.

Every Monday Mama loaded up the young'uns in the old pickup and headed into town for supplies.

The ranch road was washboard rough with holes as big as moon craters. When the truck hit a bump, up! it flew and down! it crashed with the young'uns all squealing and bouncing in the back. "Hold on to Baby!" shouted Mama. And Inez held on.

"Got to mend that road someday," Mama said. "Ain't nearly got a bone left in my body. All jarred to jelly." But there wasn't any money for mending roads.

One day in town Lorenzo spotted a poster at the general store.

CHILI COOK-OFF

WIN CASH FOR THE BEST CHILI IN WEST TEXAS

"Just the ticket," said Mama. "We'll win that contest and use the prize money to fix the ranch road. You kids can help me whip up the bestest batch of chili this side of the Mississippi."

On the day of the chili contest Mama and her young'uns got their kettle simmering and bubbling. Up and down the dusty fairgrounds folks were stirring and tasting, seasoning and spicing.

All those chili smells boiled up together in a big cloud and poured out into the sky, drifting over Que Pasa and deep into the heart of Texas. Critters and folks began to come on down to the fairgrounds, hoping for a taste.

The delicious smells floated across the West, through the hole in the ozone, and clean out into outer space, where they met up with a lean, mean, green space machine. When the space monster inside caught a whiff of that chili, he spun his ship around and headed straight for Texas.

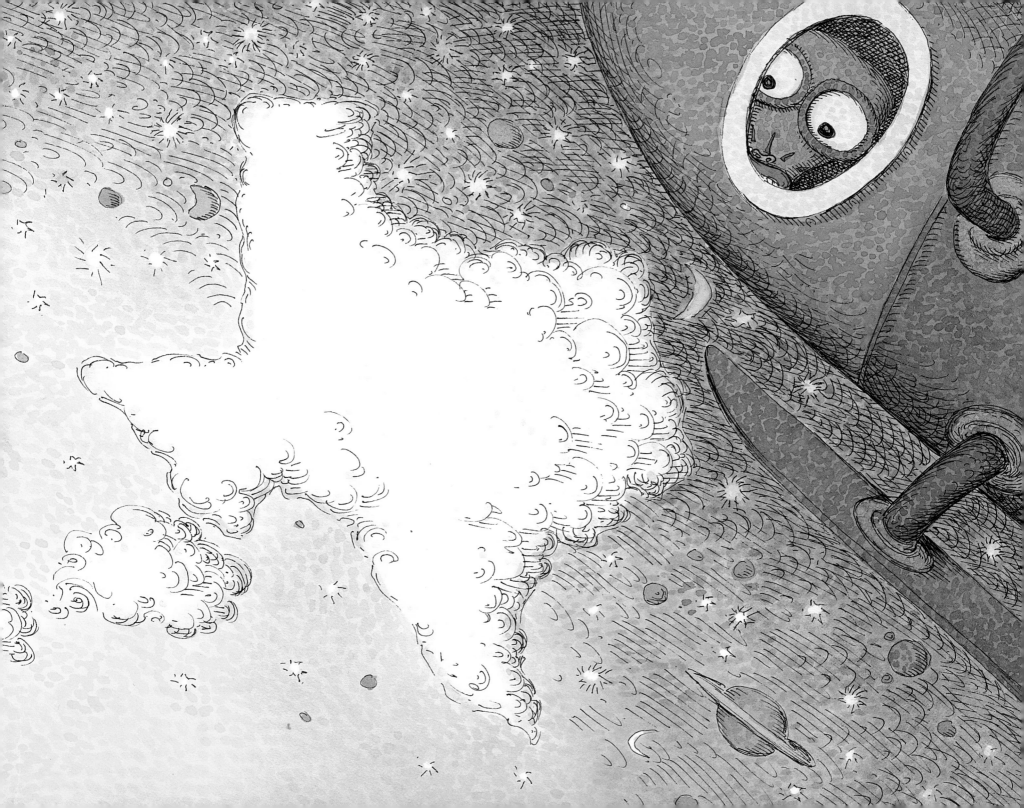

Now, Mama's recipe was a deep-down, double-dyed secret. Even Mama's young'uns didn't know what went into the pot. They held their breath as she dipped her wooden spoon into the kettle and pursed her lips to taste. "Needs a mite of SOMETHING," she said, and she shook SOMETHING into the pot from a big red box. She stirred and tasted again. "Not bad," she said. "But it needs to be rip-roarin', rootin'-tootin', rip-snortin' chili to win this cook-off." And she shook a bit more from the red box.

The young'uns watched Mama work her magic. When she was done, she walked off to rest for a spell. Inez took a sip. She frowned and added just a pinch of hot jalapeño. Lorenzo crept up to the pot. "Not so hot," he said, licking his finger. He stirred in a bit of extra-strength chili powder.

Isabel tasted. "Ain't up to snuff."
She dumped in a bottle of powerful
Tabasco.

Alfonse licked the spoon. "Just
don't cut it," he said with a sigh, as
he poured in a whole box of fiery
cayenne.

"Let me taste!" demanded Alma. Inez held her up. "It ain't purely hot enough!" Alma said. And she dropped in the string of dried chili peppers she wore around her neck.

By then Baby was crawling over. "Me want chili!" she cried, but Inez scooped her out of harm's way.

When Mama returned, she didn't have time for one last taste. The judging had begun. Mama stood behind her kettle, young'uns gathered close, all holding their breath as they watched the judges.

Meanwhile, out on the fairway, the space monster landed his ship and trotted off in search of chili. He stopped at every booth, picked up each kettle and pot in his fuzzy purple paws, and slurped down the contents.

BURP! He scarfed down Double-Strength Chili and Mite-E-Fine Chili. He lapped up Texas-Stump-Water Chili and Chock-Full-of-Chili. And still he went on. Folks were scrambling here and there, diving under their booths and cars to get out of his way.

Just as the judges were about to taste Mama's chili, the monster reached her booth. Mama and her young'uns froze. The three judges hit the dirt, hiding under Mama's apron and shaking like gelatin. The monster grabbed Mama's kettle, lifted it to his lips, and drained every last drop.

SIZZZ!!! His green eyes bugged out and his horns popped. His whiskers curled right up and **PING!** straightened right out. He quivered and he shivered and he quaked. Folks stared, wide-eyed, to see what he'd do next.

Ever so slowly, a red tongue curled out of his mouth and licked a circle around his rubbery lips. Then a grin as big as Texas stretched clean across his face. And quicker than a jackrabbit, the monster bounded off back down the fairway.

"Well, don't that beat all," the short judge said, as he and the other two judges edged out from behind Mama. The tall judge lifted his spoon for a sip of Mama's chili. But the kettle was empty. Not one single, solitary, itty-bitty drop remained.

The judges made a huddle and yelled and argued and carried on among themselves. Then they announced the winners of the Great Chili Cook-Off. Alfonse groaned as they handed out the prize money to the Stump-Water Chili cook. "We shoulda won, Mama," he said.

"Well, we gave it our bestest try, kids," said Mama. "Can't please the judges if you can't feed the judges."

Just then the middle-sized judge called everyone back. "We've decided to award a special prize. First place for showmanship goes to — Mama's Chili!"

The crowd cheered. Lorenzo gave his bestest rebel yell. Even the coyotes howled.

"Sorry there ain't no prize money with this award," said the tall judge. "Just a ribbon."

"A ribbon's all well and good," said Inez a few minutes later, "but you can't fix the ranch road with it."

"Lookit!" Alma exclaimed, spotting the monster trotting back down the fairway toward them.

"What's he want?" grumbled Alfonse. "He's already eaten all our chili!"

The monster handed Mama a kettle full of green bubbling goo. "Chee-lee," he said.

"Thank you kindly." Mama took the kettle, but she looked puzzled.

"Ugh!" said Isabel, pinching her nose, but she said it softly so Mama wouldn't hear. Mama didn't hold well with being rude, not even to strange monsters.

"I know what it is!" shouted Inez. "It's Outer Space Chili! He liked ours best, so he's giving us some of his. It must be his way of saying 'Howdy!'"

The monster grinned and tooted through his horns. Then he lit out down the fairway again, climbed into his ship, and sailed out of sight.

"Hope he didn't expect us to eat this," said Lorenzo. He stuck his finger in the goo and sniffed. "It's as sticky as tar. Smells like it, too."

"Tar!" exclaimed Mama. "Why, that gives me an idea! Quick, young'uns, before it cools!" In short order, they had all their stuff stowed in the pickup and were on their way home.

When they got to the ranch road, they
stopped at each pothole and ladled out some
Outer Space Chili. Soon all the holes were filled with green goo.
When it cooled, it dried hard as an iron skillet, just as Mama had suspected.

Tuesday night is still chili night at Mama's. She's opened her own restaurant, making money hand over fist, what with all the folks driving the new road from town just to taste her chicken and dumplings and barbecued ribs.

And of course her chili. The bestest in the land. Maybe even the bestest in the whole universe.